Hattie the Dancing Hippo

Jillian Powell
and Emma Dodson

Evans

Hattie wanted to dance.

She tried ballet.

No-one could lift her.

9

She tried ballroom.

No-one would dance with her.

13

She tried tap…

...then jive.

"I'll never be a dancer," Hattie thought.

She tried one more class.

21

She wobbled.

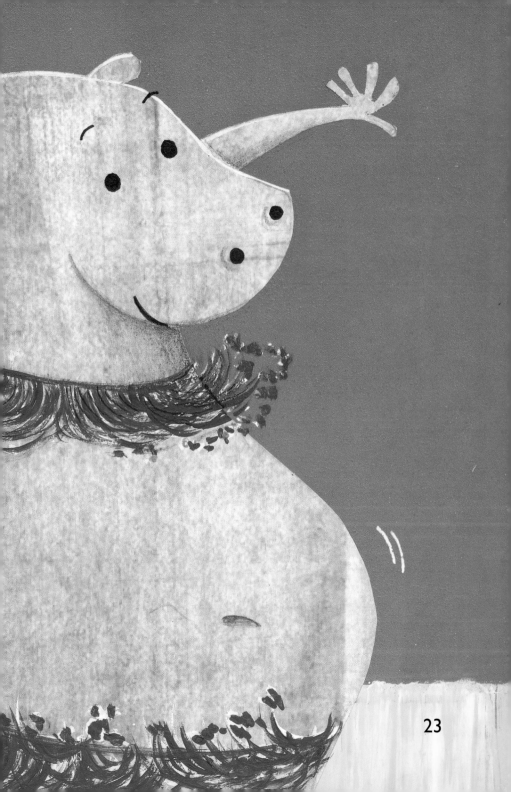

23

She wiggled.

She waggled.

Hattie was belly-dancing.

29

She was the best in class!

31

Why not try reading another Twisters book?